DUNCAN'S WAY

IAN WALLACE

A GROUNDWOOD BOOK   DOUGLAS & McINTYRE   TORONTO   VANCOUVER

Groundwood Books/Douglas & McIntyre
720 Bathurst Street, Suite 500
Toronto, Ontario M5S 2R4

We acknowledge the financial support of the Canada Council for the Arts, the
Ontario Arts Council and the Government of Canada through the Book
Publishing Industry Development Program for our publishing activities.

Canadian Cataloguing in Publication Data

Wallace, Ian, 1950-
Duncan's way
1st Canadian ed.
"A Groundwood book."
ISBN 0-88899-388-9
I. Title.
PS8595.A566D86 2000   jC813'.54   C99-932963-4
PZ7.W1562Du 2000

Book design by Annemarie Redmond
The illustrations for this book were created with watercolour.
Printed and bound in China by Everbest Printing Co. Ltd.

For the Major family, with affection and gratitude

FOR SEVEN GENERATIONS THE MEN of Duncan's family fished in broad wooden boats off the coast of Newfoundland. Painted the colours of sealskin, fresh cream or lupins in June, the longliners were christened with the names of the women whom the fishermen loved. But the boats no longer returned with their holds laden. The days of plenty were over. The cod had disappeared from the ocean's depths, and with them went a way of life.

Duncan and his father stood watching a lone kittiwake circle the abandoned fishing stages that dotted the shore.

"C'mon, Dad," he said. "Let's go do something. Anything."

There was no reply. In the eighteen months that his father had been out of work, Duncan often found him just staring at the sea.

"Didya hear me, Dad?"

"Yeah, sorry. Not now. Maybe later."

"Yeah. Like maybe January when the snow's flying around our ears."

Duncan stormed from the yard, past the empty homes of friends and neighbours who had packed up and moved away. Beyond the windswept church, he stopped where the cemetery rolled to the sea. He came here whenever he needed to sort things out. He wasn't afraid to be among the graves.

He crouched low, his fingers tracing the chiselled letters on his great-grandfather's headstone. Then he took a harmonica from his pocket and played an old fishing song.

His dad hadn't always been silent and sad. Mostly Duncan remembered him whistling and singing and joking and teasing. But that was before the foreign factory ships had sucked the cod from the ocean. Or the seals had swallowed them up. Or men like his father had overfished the stocks. Or whatever reason you believed about why the fish were gone.

He confronted the North Atlantic. "My dad was born to the sea. Like his father and all the fathers before him." He smacked the harmonica against the palm of his hand. "I'm gonna get him back there!"

When he returned home his dad was sitting on the sofa, watching a game show on TV. Some guy had just won a huge jackpot and was going wild. Duncan could tell his father was envious.

Without warning, Luke, his brother, snuck up behind him.

"Go out for a little one-on-one, dipstick?" he whispered, and bounced a basketball off Duncan's back.

"You're not the boss of me!" He jabbed his brother hard in the ribs.

Luke laughed. "Ooh, tough guy!" The ball whizzed by Duncan's ear. It hit the far wall with a solid smack, dropped to the floor and bounced around the room. Their father didn't look away from the TV. He just put another handful of popcorn into his mouth.

His mother came through the back door from her job at the grocery store.

"Oh, do these little piggies ache," she said, kicking off her shoes. She gave Duncan a hug. "And how is my little fella?"

Duncan groaned. "I'm not your little fella, Mom. I'm eleven and a half." He started to pull away.

She kissed the top of his head. "You'll always be my little fella."

While his mother fixed supper, Duncan set the table.

"I was thinking about Dad," he told her. "About how he needs to get back to the sea."

"That won't happen for a long time, my son. Nobody knows when there'll be enough cod to fish again." She flipped thick slices of bologna in the sputtering pan.

"But he does nothing except watch TV or stand at the side of the road talking to his buddies." His mother's body tensed. Duncan's eyes scanned the six loaves of bread on the counter. The four partridgeberry pies. And the plate of tea buns. "And bake."

"Baking is hard work, too!" she snapped, and turned off the stove. "Supper's ready."

When the dishes were done, Duncan and his mother and brother went up the shore. The largest iceberg they could remember had floated into the bay and grounded. It sat so naturally there, shimmering in the darkening water, that Duncan hoped it would never melt away. In the quiet, his mother spoke.

"You were right, Duncan. We need to get your father back to work. Lord knows, I've tried to think of every possible way. So's he." She looked out at the iceberg. Tears welled in her eyes. "Your dad and I have decided to leave Newfoundland."

The words were finally out. The ones Duncan had been dreading. The same words that many of his friends had heard before their families packed up and left the province. "There's no future for us here," they'd said.

Duncan tried to speak. To his surprise, words wouldn't come. He turned to Luke for help, but his brother looked like a guy who'd had the wind knocked out of him.

"We can begin again in another part of Canada," she said. "Just like your friends."

Duncan couldn't imagine giving up the sea for flat fields of grain, city skyscrapers or snow-covered tundra. And he couldn't imagine his father doing it, either.

"Lots of people are finding ways to stay," Luke blurted. "Bud Penney turned his garage into a video store."

"And lots haven't," she replied sadly.

Duncan regained his voice. "We can't leave. We've lived here forever."

"We don't have much choice. Time and money are running out."

Duncan slept fitfully that night. His stomach began churning when he thought of moving away. But mostly he thought about his father's boat and the boats of all the cod fishermen sitting idle at the wharves. He imagined countless others in outports strung along the coast like knots on a fishing line. All of them sat idle, too.

Early the next morning Duncan untied a dory from its mooring and, starting the motor, set out across the bay. The cold saltwater was rough beneath the boat, swelling and splashing over the hull, clean across his face.

Finally he reached the far side.

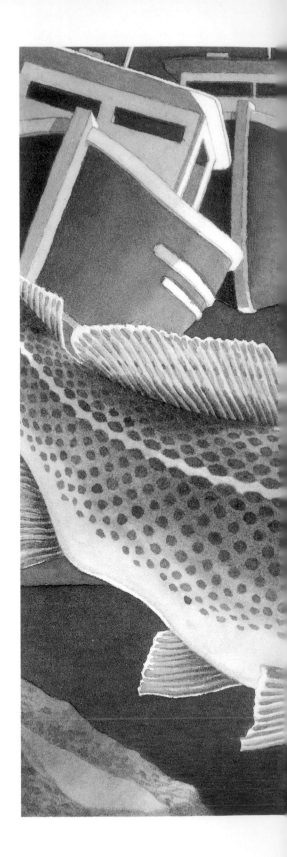

He arrived at the home of Mr. Marshall. Over several summers he and the retired fisherman had jigged for cod and played their harmonicas together. Duncan found him in the basement working on his model trains, one of them a replica of the *Newfie Bullet*, which no longer existed.

Duncan watched with delight as two trains sped through vast forests before scaling cliffs that snaked along the coastline.

Mr. Marshall gave him a turn at the controls. With the blast of an air horn the locomotives slowly gathered steam. Everything Duncan had been thinking about for the past eighteen months spilled out of him like a dam bursting.

"The disappearance of the cod is affecting us all," Mr. Marshall said when Duncan stopped talking. "I don't know that you, or I, or anyone can get your dad back to sea."

Mr. Marshall got down from his stool. He motioned Duncan to follow. They circled the miniature landscape. Then suddenly Mr. Marshall hit the ocean with his fist, picked up a tiny wooden boat and tossed it to Duncan, who caught it on the fly.

"What is a boat, if not for fishing?" he asked.

Duncan turned the boat in his fingers. "It's a way to get from place to place. Or a way of taking things to people. Or people to things."

"Darn right!" said Mr. Marshall, and he thumped his fist on the ocean a second time. The trains sped past, heading in opposite directions. A steam whistle blew. "So, boy, if there aren't any cod to fish, what do people need that your dad can take to them by boat?"

That was the toughest question Mr. Marshall had ever asked him. Duncan was lost for an answer.

"I told you, my dad does nothing except watch TV or talk to his buddies." Mr. Marshall looked disappointed. Duncan's face flushed red with embarrassment. "And bake things we love to eat. Mom says he's the best baker in the province."

Mr. Marshall nodded. "So...?"

Duncan didn't know what to say. A harmonica began to play in his head. Then he heard Luke's voice: "Lots of people are finding ways to stay." The trains slowed to a halt.

Mr. Marshall moved along the coast. He unloaded baggage and parcels, mailbags and lumber from the boxcars at two outports. His face bore the same contented look that Duncan's father got when he was baking.

"If a garage can be a video store," Duncan began slowly, "can a boat be..." He set the tiny fishing boat back in the ocean. "A bakery?"

Mr. Marshall smiled. "Possibly."

As he headed home the wind off the North Atlantic stilled. The waters of the bay became calmer. And Duncan's plan became clearer. Excitedly he revved the motor and swung wide around the iceberg.

His family was sitting at the kitchen table when he raced through the door. He brought a map from his bedroom. He traced the coastline, stopping at each outport. Slowly, thoughtfully, Duncan revealed his plan. He saw his brother's eyes brighten.

"We could stop at a different place every day," he told them.

"A bakery boat?" His mother tried out the words.

"There's bound to be at least one folk festival up the shore this summer," Luke offered. "And think of all the family reunions. That crowd from the mainland sure would be hungry."

Duncan leaned closer to his father. "If you bake it, Dad, we'll sell it from the docks."

The boys were silent, waiting for him to say something. Anything.

"A bakery boat, John?" his mother said.

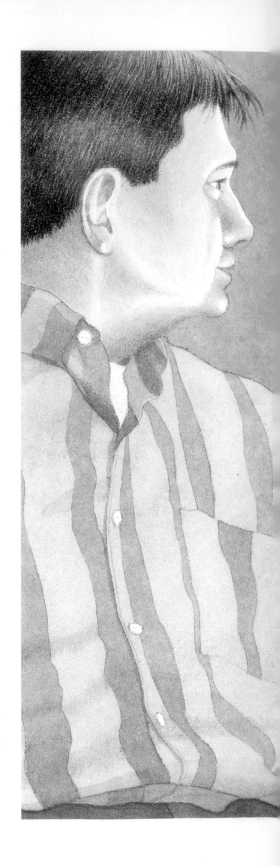

"It's not a bad idea," he said finally. "Maybe we'll have to give it a try. See if we can make a go of it." He gave Duncan a wink. He looked out the window. "By sea."

In the days that followed, Duncan's family visited every outport along the eastern shore to plot a baker's route. They went to the bank, where they took out the last of their savings and secured a loan to turn his father's boat into a floating bakery. They outfitted it with a secondhand oven and stove, a refrigerator and freezer, and all the gadgets and utensils that a baker would need. They painted the longliner from bow to stern the colours of a buttercup, and changed its name from *Barbara's Pride* to *Duncan's Way*.

Duncan painted a large sign in bold letters that said BREAD 'N' BUNS BY BOAT.

One clear July morning, they got out of bed when fishermen normally rise. Their family and friends saw them off. They set sail with a light wind at their backs. Duncan's mother was at the wheel, guiding them down the rocky coast. Duncan and Luke helped their father knead dough for bread and buns, mix batter for cakes and roll pastry for pies.

"We'll make a great team, boys," their father said as he put the first loaves into the oven.

Duncan played an old fishing song on his harmonica. His family sang boisterously along. And they joked and teased one another just like they did in the days before the cod went away.